LOCKED DOORS

BY

MARY
ROBERTS
RINEHART

BLACKBIRD BOOKS
NEW YORK • LOS ANGELES

A Blackbird Classic, February 2024

Manufactured in the United States of America.

The events and characters depicted in this book are
fictional.

Cataloging-in-Publication Data

Rinehart, Mary Roberts.
Locked doors / Mary Roberts Rinehart.
p. cm.
1. Detective and mystery stories.
2. Nurses—Fiction.
3. Women detectives—Fiction. I. Title.
PS3535.I73 L63 2024 813'.54—dc23 2024931295

Blackbird Books
www.bbirdbooks.com
email us at editor@bbirdbooks.com

ISBN 978-1-61053-045-3

First Blackbird Edition

10 9 8 7 6 5 4 3 2 1

LOCKED DOORS

I

"You promised," I reminded Mr. Patton, "to play with cards on the table."

"My dear young lady," he replied, "I have no cards! I suspect a game, that's all."

"Then—do you need me?"

The detective bent forward, his arms on his desk, and looked me over carefully.

"What sort of shape are you in? Tired?"

"No."

"Nervous?"

"Not enough to hurt."

"I want you to take another case, following a nurse who has gone to pieces," he said, selecting his words carefully. "I don't want to tell you a lot—I want you to go in with a fresh mind. It promises to be an extraordinary case."

"How long was the other nurse there?"

"Four days."

"She went to pieces in four days!"

"Well, she's pretty much unstrung. The worst is, she hasn't any real reason. A family chooses to live in an unusual manner, because they like it, or perhaps they're afraid of something. The girl was, that's sure. I had never seen her until this morning, a big, healthy-looking young woman; but she came in looking back over her shoulder as if she expected a knife in her back. She said she was a nurse from St. Luke's and that she'd been on a case for four days. She'd left that morning after about three hours' sleep in that time, being locked in a room most of the time, and having little but crackers and milk for food. She thought it was a case for the police."

"Who is ill in the house? Who was her patient?"

"There is no illness, I believe. The French governess had gone, and they wished the children competently cared for until they replaced her. That was the reason given her when she went. Afterward she—well, she was puzzled."

"How are you going to get me there?"

He gathered acquiescence from my question and smiled approval.

"Good girl!" he said. "Never mind how I'll get you there. You are the most dependable woman I know."

"The most curious, perhaps?" I retorted. "Four days on the case, three hours' sleep, locked in and yelling *Police!* Is it out of town?"

"No, in the heart of the city, on Beauregard Square. Can you get some St. Luke's uniforms? They want another St. Luke's nurse."

I said I could get the uniforms, and he wrote the address on a card.

"Better arrive about five," he said.

"But—if they are not expecting me?"

"They will be expecting you," he replied enigmatically.

"The doctor, if he's a St. Luke's man—"

"There is no doctor."

It was six months since I had solved, or helped to solve, the mystery of the buckled bag for Mr. Patton. I had had other cases for him in the interval, cases where the police could not get close enough. As I said when I began this record of my crusade against crime and the criminal, a trained nurse gets under the very skin of the soul. She finds a mind surrendered, all the crooked little motives that have fired the guns of life revealed in their pitifulness.

Gradually, I had come to see that Mr. Patton's point of view was right; that if the criminal uses every means against society, why not society against the criminal? At first I had used this as a flag of truce to my nurse's ethical training; now I flaunted it, a mental and moral banner. The criminal against society, and I against the criminal! And, more than that, against misery, healing pain by augmenting it sometimes, but working like a surgeon, for good.

I had had six cases in six months. Only in one had I failed to land my criminal, and that without any suspicion of my white uniform and rubber-soled shoes. Although I played a double game, no patient of mine had suffered. I was a nurse first and a police agent second. If it was a question between turpentine compresses—stupes, professionally—and seeing what letters came in or went out of the house, the compress went on first, and cracking hot too.

I am not boasting. That is my method, the only way I can work, and it speaks well for it that, as I say, only one man escaped arrest—an arson case where the factory owner hanged himself in the bathroom needle shower in the house he had bought with the insurance money, while I was fixing his breakfast tray. And even he might have been saved for justice had the cook not burned the toast and been obliged to make it fresh.

I was no longer staying at a nurses' home. I had taken a bachelor suite of three rooms and bath, comfortably downtown. I cooked my own breakfasts when I was off duty, and I dined at a restaurant near. Luncheon I did not bother much about. Now and then, Mr. Patton telephoned me, and we lunched together in remote places where we would not be known. He would tell me of his cases, and sometimes he asked my advice.

I bought my uniforms that day and took them home in a taxicab. The dresses were blue, and over them, for the street, the St. Luke's girls wear long cloaks, English fashion, of navy blue serge, and a blue bonnet with a white ruching and white lawn ties. I felt curious in it, but it was becoming and convenient. Certainly I looked professional.

At three o'clock that afternoon, a messenger brought a small box, registered. It contained a St. Luke's badge of gold and blue enamel.

At four o'clock my telephone rang. I was packing my suitcase according to the list I keep pasted in the lid. Under the list, which was of uniforms, aprons, thermometer, instruments, a nurse's simple set of probe, forceps, and bandage scissors, was the word "box." This always went in first—a wooden box with a lock, the key of which was round my neck. It contained skeleton keys, a small black revolver of which I was in deadly fear, a pair of handcuffs, a pocket flashlight, and my badge from the chief of police. I was examining the revolver nervously when the telephone rang, and I came within an ace of sending a bullet into the flat below.

Did you ever notice how much you get out of a telephone voice? We can dissemble with our faces, but under stress the vocal cords seem to draw up tight and the voice comes thin and colorless. There's a little woman in the flat beneath—the one I nearly bombarded—who sings like a bird at her piano half the day, scaling vocal heights that make me dizzy. Now and then, she has a visitor, a nice young man, and she disgraces herself, flats F, fogs E even, finally takes cowardly refuge in a wretched mezzo-soprano, and cries herself to sleep, doubtless, later on.

The man who called me had the thin-drawn voice of extreme strain—a youngish voice.

"Miss Adams," he said, "this is Francis Reed speaking. I have called St. Luke's and they referred me to you. Are you free to take a case this afternoon?"

I fenced. I was trying to read the voice.

"This afternoon?"

"Well, before night anyhow; as—as early this evening as possible."

The voice was strained and tired, desperately tired. It was not peevish. It was even rather pleasant.

"What is the case, Mr. Reed?"

He hesitated. "It is not illness. It is merely—the governess has gone and there are two small children. We want someone to give her undivided attention to the children."

"I see."

"Are you a heavy sleeper, Miss Adams?"

"A very light one." I fancied he breathed freer.

"I hope you are not tired from a previous case?"

I was beginning to like the voice.

"I'm quite fresh," I replied almost gaily. "Even if I were not, I like children, especially well ones. I shan't find looking after them very wearying, I'm sure."

Again the odd little pause. Then he gave me the address on Beauregard Square, and asked me to be sure not to be late.

"I must warn you," he added; "we are living in a sort of casual way. Our servants left us without warning. Mrs. Reed has been getting along as best she could. Most of our meals are being sent in."

I was thinking fast. No servants! A good many people think a trained nurse is a sort of upper servant. I've been in houses where they were amazed to discover that I was a college woman and, finding the two things irreconcilable, have openly accused me of having been driven to such a desperate course as a hospital training by an unfortunate love affair.

"Of course you understand that I will look after the children to the best of my ability, but that I will not replace the servants."

I fancied he smiled grimly.

"That of course. Will you ring twice when you come?"

"Ring twice?"

"The doorbell," he replied impatiently.

I said I would ring the doorbell twice.

The young woman below was caroling gaily, ignorant of the six-barreled menace over her head. I knelt again by my suitcase, but packed little and thought a great deal. I was to arrive before dusk at a house where there were no servants and to ring the doorbell twice. I was to be a light sleeper, although I was to look after two healthy children. It was not much in itself, but, taken in connection with the previous nurse's appeal to the police, it took on new possibilities.

At six I started out to dinner. It was early spring and cold, but quite light. At the first corner, I saw Mr. Patton waiting for a street car, and at his quick nod, I saw I was to get in also. He did not pay my fare or speak to me. It was a part of the game that we were never seen together except at the remote restaurant I mentioned before. The car thinned out and I could watch him easily. Far downtown, he alighted, and so did I. The restaurant was near. I went in alone and sat down at a table in a recess, and very soon he joined me. We were in the main dining room but not of it, a sop at once to the conventions and to the necessity, where he was so well known, for caution.

"I got a little information—on—the affair we were talking of," he said as he sat down. "I'm not so sure I want you to take the case after all."

"Certainly I shall take it," I retorted with some sharpness. "I've promised to go."

"Tut! I'm not going to send you into danger unnecessarily."

"I am not afraid."

"Exactly. A lot of generals were lost in the Civil War because they were not afraid and wanted to lead their troops instead of saving themselves and their expensive West Point training by sitting back in a safe spot and directing the fight. Any fool can run into danger. It takes intellect to keep out."

I felt my color rising indignantly.

"Then you brought me here to tell me I am not to go?"

"Will you let me read you two reports?"

"You could have told me that at the corner!"

"Will you let me read you two reports?"

"If you don't mind, I'll first order something to eat. I'm to be there before dark."

"Will you let me—"

"I'm going, and you know I'm going. If you don't want me to represent you, I'll go on my own. They want a nurse, and they're in trouble."

I think he was really angry. I know I was. If there is anything that takes the very soul out of a woman, it is to be kept from doing a thing she has set her heart on, because some man thinks it danger-ous. If she has any spirit, that rouses it.

Mr. Patton quietly replaced the reports in his wallet, and his wallet in the inside pocket of his coat, and fell to a judicial survey of the menu. But, although he did not even glance at me, he must have felt the determination in my face, for he ordered things that were quickly prepared and told the waiter to hurry.

"I have wondered lately," he said slowly, "whether the mildness of your manner at the hospital was acting, or the chastening effect of three years under an order book."

"A man always likes a woman to be a sheep."

"Not at all. But it is rather disconcerting to have a pet lamb turn round and take a bite out of one."

"Will you read the reports now?"

"I think," he said quietly, "they would better wait until we have eaten. We will probably both feel calmer. Suppose we arrange that nothing said before the oysters counts?"

I agreed, rather sulkily, and the meal went off well enough. I was anxious enough to hurry but he ate deliberately, drank his demi-tasse, paid the waiter, and at last met my impatient eyes and smiled.

"After all," he said, "since you are determined to go anyhow, what's the use of reading the reports? Inside of an hour, you'll know all you need to know." But he saw that I did not take his teasing well, and drew out his pocketbook.

They were two typewritten papers clamped together.

They are on my desk before me now. The first one is endorsed:

Statement by Laura J. Bosworth, nurse, of St. Luke's Home for Graduate Nurses.

Miss Bosworth says:

I do not know just why I came here. But I know I'm frightened. That's the fact. I think there is something terribly wrong in the house of Francis M. Reed, 71 Beauregard Square. I think a crime of some sort has been committed. There are four people in the family, Mr. and Mrs. Reed and two children. I was to look after the children.

I was there four days and the children were never allowed out of the room. At night, we were locked in. I kept wondering what I would do if there was a fire. The telephone wires are cut so no one can call the house, and I believe the doorbell is disconnected too. But that's fixed now. Mrs. Reed went round all the time with a face like chalk and her eyes staring. At all hours of the night, she'd unlock the bedroom door and come in and look at the children.

Almost all the doors through the house were locked. If I wanted to get to the kitchen to boil eggs for the children's breakfast—for there were no servants, and Mrs. Reed was young and didn't know anything about cooking—Mr. Reed had to unlock about four doors for me.

If Mrs. Reed looked bad, he was dreadful—sunken-eyed and white and wouldn't eat. I think he has killed somebody and is making away with the body.

Last night, I said I had to have air, and they let me go out. I called up a friend from a pay station, another nurse. This morning she sent me a special delivery letter that I was needed on another case, and I got away. That's all; it sounds foolish, but try it and see if it doesn't get on your nerves.

Mr. Patton looked up at me as he finished reading.

"Now you see what I mean," he said. "That woman was there four days, and she is as temperamental as a cow, but in those four days her nervous system went to smash."

"Doors locked!" I reflected. "Servants gone; state of fear—it looks like a siege!"

"But why a trained nurse? Why not a policeman, if there is danger? Why anyone at all, if there is something that the police are not to know?"

"That is what I intend to find out," I replied. He shrugged his shoulders and read the other paper:

Report of Detective Bennett on Francis M. Reed, April 5, 1913:

Francis M. Reed is thirty-six years of age, married, a chemist at the Olympic Paint Works. He has two children, both boys. Has a small independent income and owns the house on Beauregard Square, which was built by his grandfather, General F. R. Reed. Is supposed to be living beyond his means. House is usually full of servants, and grocer in the neighborhood has had to wait for money several times.

On March twenty-ninth, he dismissed all servants without warning. No reason given, but a week's wages instead of notice.

On March thirtieth, he applied to the owners of the paint factory for two weeks' vacation. Gave as his reason nervousness and insomnia. He said he was "going to lay off and get some sleep." Has not been back at the works since. House under surveillance this afternoon. No visitors.

Mr. Reed telephoned for a nurse at four o'clock from a store on Eleventh Street. Explained that his telephone was out of order.

Mr. Patton folded up the papers and thrust them back into his pocket. Evidently he saw I was determined, for he only said:

"Have you got your revolver?"

"Yes."

"Do you know anything about telephones? Could you repair that one in an emergency?"

"In an emergency," I retorted, "there is no time to repair a telephone. But I've got a voice and there are windows. If I really put my mind to it, you will hear me yell at headquarters."

He smiled grimly.

II

The Reed house is on Beauregard Square. It is a small, exclusive community, the Beauregard neighborhood; a dozen or more solid citizens built their homes there in the early '70's, occupying large lots, the houses flush with the streets and with gardens behind. Six on one street, six on another, back-to-back with the gardens in the center, they occupied the whole block. And the gardens were not fenced off, but made a sort of small park unsuspected from the streets. Here and there, bits of flowering shrubbery sketchily outlined a property, but the general impression was of lawn and trees, free of access to all the owners. Thus, with the square in front and the gardens in the rear, the Reed house faced in two directions on the early spring green.

In the gardens, the old tar walks were still there, and a fountain which no longer played, but on whose stone coping I believe the young Beauregard Squarites made their first climbing ventures.

The gardens were always alive with birds, and later, on from my windows, I learned the reason. It seems to have been a custom sanctified by years, that the crumbs from the twelve tables should be thrown into the dry basin of the fountain for the birds. It was a common sight to see stately butlers and chic little waitresses in black and white coming out after luncheon or dinner with silver trays of crumbs. Many a scrap of gossip, as well as scrap of food, has been passed along at the old stone fountain, I believe. I know that it was there that I heard of the basement ghost of Beauregard Square—a whisper at first, a panic later.

I arrived at eight o'clock and rang the doorbell twice. The door was opened at once by Mr. Reed, a tall, blond young man carefully dressed. He threw away his cigarette when he saw me and shook hands. The hall was brightly lighted and most cheerful; in fact the whole house was ablaze with light. Certainly nothing could be less mysterious than the house, or

than the debonair young man who motioned me into
the library.

"I told Mrs. Reed I would talk to you before you
go upstairs," he said. "Will you sit down?"

I sat down. The library was even brighter than
the hall, and now I saw that although he smiled as
cheerfully as ever, his face was almost colorless, and
his eyes, which looked frankly enough into mine for
a moment, went wandering off round the room. I
had the impression somehow that Mr. Patton had
had of the nurse at headquarters that morning—that
he looked as if he expected a knife in his back. It
seemed to me that he wanted to look over his shoulder and by sheer willpower did not.

"You know the rule, Miss Adams," he said:
"When there's an emergency get a trained nurse. I
told you our emergency—no servants and two small
children."

"This should be a good time to secure servants,"
I said briskly. "City houses are being deserted for
country places, and a percentage of servants won't
leave town."

He hesitated.

"We've been doing very nicely, although of
course it's hardly more than just living. Our meals are
sent in from a hotel, and—well, we thought, since we

are going away so soon, that perhaps we could manage."

The impulse was too strong for him at that moment. He wheeled and looked behind him, not a hasty glance, but a deliberate inspection that took in every part of that end of the room. It was so unexpected that it left me gasping.

The next moment he was himself again.

"When I say that there is no illness," he said, "I am hardly exact. There is no illness, but there has been an epidemic of children's diseases among the Beauregard Square children and we are keeping the youngsters indoors."

"Don't you think they could be safeguarded without being shut up in the house?"

He responded eagerly.

"If I only thought—" he checked himself. "No," he said decidedly; "for a time at least I believe it is not wise."

I did not argue with him. There was nothing to be gained by antagonizing him. And as Mrs. Reed came in just then, the subject was dropped. She was hardly more than a girl, almost as blond as her husband, very pretty, and with the weariest eyes I have ever seen, unless perhaps the eyes of a man who has waited a long time for deathly tuberculosis.

I liked her at once. She did not attempt to smile. She rather clung to my hand when I held it out.

"I am glad St. Luke's still trusts us," she said. "I was afraid the other nurse— Frank, will you take Miss Adams' suitcase upstairs?"

She held out a key. He took it, but he turned at the door:

"I wish you wouldn't wear those things, Anne. You gave me your promise yesterday, you remember."

"I can't work round the children in anything else," she protested.

"Those things" were charming. She wore a rose silk negligee trimmed with soft bands of lace and blue satin flowers, a petticoat to match that garment, and a lace cap.

He hesitated in the doorway and looked at her— a curious glance, I thought, full of tenderness, reproof—apprehension perhaps.

"I'll take it off, dear," she replied to the glance. "I wanted Miss Adams to know that, even if we haven't a servant in the house, we are at least civilized. I—I haven't taken cold." This last was clearly an afterthought.

He went out then and left us together. She came over to me swiftly.

"What did the other nurse say?" she demanded.

"I do not know her at all. I have not seen her."

"Didn't she report at the hospital that we were—queer?"

I smiled.

"That's hardly likely, is it?"

Unexpectedly she went to the door opening into the hall and closed it, coming back swiftly.

"Mr. Reed thinks it is not necessary, but—there are some things that will puzzle you. Perhaps I should have spoken to the other nurse. If—if anything strikes you as unusual, Miss Adams, just please don't see it! It is all right, everything is all right. But something has occurred—not very much, but disturbing—and we are all of us doing the very best we can."

She was quivering with nervousness.

I was not the police agent then, I'm afraid.

"Nurses are accustomed to disturbing things. Perhaps I can help."

"You can, by watching the children. That's the only thing that matters to me—the children. I don't want them left alone. If you have to leave them call me."

"Don't you think I will be able to watch them more intelligently if I know just what the danger is?"

I think she very nearly told me. She was so tired, evidently so anxious to shift her burden to fresh shoulders.

"Mr. Reed said," I prompted her, "that there was an epidemic of children's diseases. But from what you say—"

But I was not to learn, after all, for her husband opened the hall door.

"Yes, children's diseases," she said vaguely. "So many children are down. Shall we go up, Frank?"

The extraordinary bareness of the house had been dawning on me for some time. It was well lighted and well furnished. But the floors were innocent of rugs, the handsome furniture was without arrangement, and, in the library at least, stood huddled in the center of the room. The hall and stairs were also uncarpeted, but there were marks where carpets had recently lain and had been jerked up.

The progress up the staircase was not calculated to soothe my nerves. The thought of my little revolver, locked in my suitcase, was poor comfort. For with every four steps or so, Mr. Reed, who led the way, turned automatically and peered into the hallway below; he was listening, too, his head bent slightly forward. And each time that he turned, his wife behind me turned also. Cold terror suddenly got me by the spine, and yet the hall was bright with light.

(Note: Surely fear is a contagion. Could one isolate the germ of it and find an antitoxin? Or is it merely a form of nervous activity run amuck, like a runaway locomotive, colliding with other nervous activities and causing catastrophe? Take this up with Mr. Patton. But would he know? He, I am almost sure, has never been really afraid.)

I had a vision of my ox-like predecessor making this head-over-shoulder journey up the staircase, and, in spite of my nervousness, I smiled. But at that moment, Mrs. Reed behind me put a hand on my arm, and I screamed. I remember yet the way she dropped back against the wall and turned white.

Mr. Reed whirled on me instantly.

"What did you see?" he demanded.

"Nothing at all." I was horribly ashamed. "Your wife touched my arm unexpectedly. I dare say I am nervous."

"It's all right, Anne," he reassured her. And to me, almost irritably:

"I thought you nurses had no nerves."

"Under ordinary circumstances I have none."

It was all ridiculous. We were still on the staircase.

"Just what do you mean by that?"

"If you will stop looking down into that hall I'll be calm enough. You make me jumpy."

He muttered something about being sorry and went on quickly. But at the top, he went through an inward struggle, evidently succumbed, and took a final furtive survey of the hallway below. I was so wrought up that had a door slammed anywhere just then, I think I should have dropped where I stood.

The absolute silence of the house added to the strangeness of the situation. Beauregard Square is not close to a trolley line, and quiet is the neighborhood tradition. The first rubber-tired vehicles in the city drew up before Beauregard Square houses. Beauregard Square children speak in low voices and never bang their spoons on their plates. Beauregard Square servants wear felt-soled shoes. And such outside noises as venture to intrude themselves must filter through double brick walls and doors built when lumber was selling by the thousand acres instead of the square foot.

Through this silence, our feet echoed along the bare floor of the upper hall, as well lighted as downstairs and as dismantled, to the door of the day nursery. The door was locked—double locked, in fact. For the key had been turned in the old fashioned lock, and in addition, an ordinary bolt had been newly fastened on the outside of the door. On the outside! Was that to keep me in? It was certainly not to keep anyone or anything out. The feeblest touch moved the bolt.

We were all three outside the door. We seemed to keep our compactness by common consent. No one of us left the group willingly; or, leaving it, we slid back again quickly. That was my impression, at least. But the bolt rather alarmed me.

"This is your room," Mrs. Reed said. "It is generally the day nursery, but we have put a bed and some other things in it. I hope you will be comfortable."

I touched the bolt with my finger and smiled into Mr. Reed's eyes.

"I hope I am not to be fastened in!" I said.

He looked back squarely enough, but somehow I knew he lied.

"Certainly not," he replied, and opened the door.

If there had been mystery outside, and bareness, the nursery was charming—a corner room with many windows, hung with the simplest of nursery papers and full of glass-doored closets filled with orderly rows of toys. In one corner, a small single bed had been added without spoiling the room. The windowsills were full of flowering plants. There was a bowl of goldfish on a stand, and a tiny dwarf parrot in a cage was covered against the night air by a bright afghan. A white-tiled bathroom connected with this room and also with the night nursery beyond.

Mr. Reed did not come in. I had an uneasy feeling, however, that he was just beyond the door. The children were not asleep. Mrs. Reed left me to let me put on my uniform. When she came back her face was troubled.

"They are not sleeping well," she complained. "I suppose it comes from having no exercise. They are always excited."

"I'll take their temperatures," I said. "Sometimes a tepid bath and a cup of hot milk will make them sleep."

The two little boys were wide awake. They sat up to look at me, and both spoke at once.

"Can you tell fairy tales out of your head?"

"Did you see Chang?"

They were small, sleek-headed, fair-skinned youngsters, adorably clean and rumpled.

"Chang is their dog, a Pekingese," explained the mother. "He has been lost for several days."

"But he isn't lost, mother. I can hear him crying every now and then. You'll look again, mother, won't you?"

"We heard him through the furnace pipe," shrilled the smaller of the two. "You said you would look."

"I did look, darlings. He isn't there. And you promised not to cry about him, Freddie."

Freddie, thus put on his honor, protested he was not crying for the dog.

"I want to go out and take a walk, that's why I'm crying," he wailed. "And I want Mademoiselle, and my buttons are all off. And my ear aches when I lie on it."

The room was close. I threw up the windows, and turned to find Mrs. Reed at my elbows. She was glancing out apprehensively.

"I suppose the air is necessary," she said, "and these windows are all right. But—I have a reason for asking it—please do not open the others."

She went very soon, and I listened as she went out. I had promised to lock the door behind her, and I did so. The bolt outside was not shot.

After I had quieted the children with my mildest fairy story, I made a quiet inventory of my new quarters. The rough diagram of the second floor is the one I gave Mr. Patton later. That night, of course, I investigated only the two nurseries. But, so strangely had the fear that hung over the house infected me, I confess that I made my little tour of bathroom and clothes closet with my revolver in my hand!

I found nothing, of course. The disorder of the house had not extended itself here. The bathroom was spotless with white tile; the large clothes closet which opened off the passage between the two rooms was full of neatly folded clothing for the children. The closet was to play its part later, a darkish little room faintly lighted by a ground glass transom opening into the center hall, but dependent mostly on electric light.

Outside the windows Mrs. Reed had asked me not to open was a porte-cochère roof almost level with the sills. Then was it an outside intruder she feared? And in that case, why the bolts on the outside of the two nursery doors? For the night nursery, I found, must have one also. I turned the key, but the door would not open.

I decided not to try to sleep that night, but to keep on watch. So powerfully had the mother's anxiety about her children and their mysterious danger impressed me that I made frequent excursions into the back room. Up to midnight there was nothing whatever to alarm me. I darkened both rooms and sat, waiting for I know not what; for some sound to show that the house stirred, perhaps. At a few minutes after twelve, faint noises penetrated to my room from the hall, Mr. Reed's nervous voice and a piece of furniture scraping over the floor. Then silence again for half an hour or so.

Then—I was quite certain that the bolt on my door had been shot. I did not hear it, I think. Perhaps I felt it. Perhaps I only feared it. I unlocked the door; it was fastened outside.

There is a hideous feeling of helplessness about being locked in. I pretended to myself at first that I was only interested and curious. But I was frightened; I know that now. I sat there in the dark and wondered what I would do if the house took fire, or if some hideous tragedy enacted itself outside that locked door, and I were helpless.

By two o'clock, I had worked myself into a panic. The house was no longer silent. Someone was moving about downstairs, and not stealthily. The sounds came up through the heavy joists and flooring of the old house.

I determined to make at least a struggle to free myself. There was no way to get at the bolts, of course. The porte-cochère roof remained and the transom in the clothes closet. True, I might have raised an alarm and been freed at once, but naturally, I rejected this method. The roof of the porte-cochère proved impracticable. The tin bent and cracked under my first step. The transom then.

I carried a chair into the closet and found the transom easy to lower. But it threatened to creak. I put liquid soap on the hinges—it was all I had, and it worked very well—and lowered the transom inch by inch. Even then I could not see over it. I had worked so far without a sound, but in climbing to a shelf, my foot slipped, and I thought I heard a sharp movement outside. It was five minutes before I stirred. I hung there, every muscle cramped, listening and waiting. Then I lifted myself by sheer force of muscle and looked out. The upper landing of the staircase, brilliantly lighted, was to my right. Across the head of the stairs had been pushed a cot bed, made up for the night, but it was unoccupied.

Mrs. Reed, in a long, dark ulster, was standing beside it, staring with fixed and glassy eyes at something in the lower hall.

III

Sometime after four o'clock, my door was unlocked from without; the bolt slipped as noiselessly as it had been shot. I got a little sleep until seven, when the boys trotted into my room in their bathrobes and slippers and perched on my bed.

"It's a nice day," observed Harry, the elder. "Is that bump your feet?"

I wriggled my toes and assured him he had surmised correctly.

"You're pretty long, aren't you? Do you think we can play in the fountain today?"

"We'll make a try for it, son. It will do us all good to get out into the sunshine."

"We always took Chang for a walk every day, Mademoiselle and Chang and Freddie and I."

Freddie had found my cap on the dressing table and had put it on his yellow head. But now, on hearing the beloved name of his pet, he burst into loud grief-stricken howls.

"Want Mam'selle," he cried. "Want Chang too. Poor Freddie!"

The children were adorable. I bathed and dressed them and, mindful of my predecessor's story of crackers and milk, prepared for an excursion kitchenward. The nights might be full of mystery, murder might romp from room to room, but I intended to see that the youngsters breakfasted. But before I was ready to go down, breakfast arrived.

Perhaps the other nurse had told the Reeds a few plain truths before she left; perhaps, and this I think was the case, the cloud had lifted just a little. Whatever it may have been, two rather flushed and blistered young people tapped at the door that morning and were admitted, Mr. Reed first, with a tray, Mrs. Reed following, with a coffee pot and cream.

The little nursery table was small for five, but we made room somehow. What if the eggs were underdone and the toast dry? The children munched blissfully. What if Mr. Reed's face was still drawn and haggard and his wife a limp little huddle on the floor? She sat with her head against his knee and her eyes on the little boys, and drank her pale coffee slowly. She was very tired, poor thing. She dropped asleep sitting there, and he sat for a long time, not liking to disturb her.

It made me feel homesick for the home I didn't have. I've had the same feeling before, of being a rank outsider, a sort of defrauded feeling. I've had it when I've seen the look in a man's eyes when his wife comes-to after an operation. And I've had it, for that matter, when I've put a new baby in its mother's arms for the first time. I had it for sure that morning, while she slept there and he stroked her pretty hair.

I put in my plea for the children then.

"It's bright and sunny," I argued. "And if you are nervous I'll keep them away from other children. But if you want to keep them well you must give them exercise."

It was the argument about keeping them well that influenced him, I think. He sat silent for a long time. His wife was still asleep, her lips parted.

"Very well," he said finally, "from two to three, Miss Adams. But not in the garden back of the house. Take them on the street."

I agreed to that.

"I shall want a short walk every evening myself," I added. "That is a rule of mine. I am a more useful person and a more agreeable one if I have it."

I think he would have demurred if he dared. But one does not easily deny so sane a request. He yielded grudgingly.

That first day was calm and quiet enough. Had it not been for the strange condition of the house and the necessity for keeping the children locked in, I would have smiled at my terror of the night. Luncheon was sent in; so was dinner. The children and I lunched and supped alone. As far as I could see, Mrs. Reed made no attempt at housework; but the cot at the head of the stairs disappeared in the early morning, and the dog did not howl again.

I took the boys out for an hour in the early afternoon. Two incidents occurred, both of them significant. I bought myself a screw driver—that was one. The other was our meeting with a slender young woman in black who knew the boys and stopped them. She proved to be one of the dismissed servants—the waitress, she said.

"Why, Freddie!" she cried. "And Harry too! Aren't you going to speak to Nora?"

After a moment or two she turned to me, and I felt she wanted to say something, but hardly dared.

"How is Mrs. Reed?" she asked. "Not sick, I hope?"

She glanced at my St. Luke's cloak and bonnet.

"No, she is quite well."

"And Mr. Reed?"

"Quite well also."

"Is Mademoiselle still there?"

"No, there is no one there but the family. There are no maids in the house."

She stared at me curiously.

"Mademoiselle has gone? Are you cer— Excuse me, Miss. But I thought she would never go. The children were like her own."

"She is not there, Nora."

She stood for a moment debating, I thought. Then she burst out:

"Mr. Reed made a mistake, miss. You can't take a houseful of first-class servants and dismiss them the way he did, without half an hour to get out bag and baggage, without making talk. And there's talk enough all through the neighborhood."

"What sort of talk?"

"Different people say different things. They say Mademoiselle is still there, locked in her room on the third floor. There's a light there sometimes, but nobody sees her. And other folks say Mr. Reed is crazy. And there is worse being said than that."

But she refused to tell me any more—evidently concluded she had said too much and got away as quickly as she could, looking rather worried.

I was a trifle over my hour getting back, but nothing was said. To leave the clean and tidy street for the disordered house was not pleasant. But once in the children's suite, with the goldfish in the aquarium darting like tongues of flame in the sunlight, with the tulips and hyacinths of the window boxes glowing and the orderly toys on their white shelves, I felt comforted. After all, disorder and dust did not imply crime.

But one thing I did that afternoon—did it with firmness and no attempt at secrecy, and after asking permission of no one. I took the new screw driver and unfastened the bolt from the outside of my door.

I was prepared, if necessary, to make a stand on that issue. But although it was noticed, I knew, no mention of it was made to me.

Mrs. Reed pleaded a headache that evening, and I believe her husband ate alone in the dismantled dining room. For every room on the lower floor, I had discovered, was in the same curious disorder.

At seven, Mr. Reed relieved me to go out. The children were in bed. He did not go into the day nursery, but placed a straight chair outside the door of the back room and sat there, bent over, elbows on knees, chin cupped in his palm, staring at the staircase. He roused enough to ask me to bring an evening paper when I returned.

When I am on a department case, I always take my off-duty in the evening, by arrangement, and walk round the block. Sometime in my walk, I am sure to see Mr. Patton himself, if the case is big enough, or one of his agents if he cannot come. If I have nothing to communicate, it resolves itself into a bow and nothing more.

I was nervous on this particular jaunt. For one thing, my St. Luke's cloak and bonnet marked me at once, made me conspicuous; for another, I was afraid Mr. Patton would think the Reed house no place for a woman and order me home.

It was a quarter to eight and quite dark, before he fell into step beside me.

"Well," I replied rather shakily; "I'm still alive, as you see."

"Then it is pretty bad?"

"It's exceedingly queer," I admitted, and told my story. I had meant to conceal the bolt on the outside of my door, and one or two other things, but I blurted them all out right then and there, and felt a lot better at once.

He listened intently.

"It's fear of the deadliest sort," I finished.

"Fear of the police?"

"I—I think not. It is fear of something in the house. They are always listening and watching at the top of the front stairs. They have lifted all the carpets, so that every footstep echoes through the whole house. Mrs. Reed goes down to the first door, but never alone. Today, I found that the back staircase is locked off at top and bottom. There are doors."

I gave him my rough diagram of the house. It was too dark to see it.

"It is only tentative," I explained. "So much of the house is locked up, and every movement of mine is under surveillance. Without baths, there are about twelve large rooms, counting the third floor. I've not been able to get there, but I thought that tonight I'd try to look about."

"You had no sleep last night?"

"Three hours—from four to seven this morning."

We had crossed into the public square and were walking slowly under the trees. Now he stopped and faced me.

"I don't like the look of it, Miss Adams," he said. "Ordinary panic goes and hides. But here's a fear that knows what it's afraid of and takes methodical steps for protection. I didn't want you to take the case, you know that; but now I'm not going to insult you by asking you to give it up. But I'm going to see that you are protected. There will be someone across the street every night, as long as you are in the house."

"Have you any theory?" I asked him. He is not strong for theories generally. He is very practical. "That is, do you think the other nurse was right, and there is some sort of crime being concealed?"

"Well, think about it," he prompted me. "If a murder has been committed, what are they afraid of? The police? Then why a trained nurse and all this caution about the children? A ghost? Would they lift the carpets so that they could hear the specter tramping about?"

"If there is no crime, but something—a lunatic perhaps?" I asked.

"Possibly. But then why this secrecy and keeping out the police? It is, of course, possible that your respected employers have both gone off mentally, and the whole thing is a nightmare delusion. On my word, it sounds like it. But it's too much for credulity to believe they've both gone crazy with the same form of delusion."

"Perhaps I'm the lunatic," I said despairingly. "When you reduce it like that to an absurdity, I wonder if I didn't imagine it all, the lights burning everywhere and the carpets up, and Mrs. Reed staring down the staircase, and I locked in a room and hanging on by my nails to peer out through a closet transom."

"Perhaps. But how about the deadly sane young woman who preceded you? She had no imagination. Now about Reed and his wife—how do they strike you? They get along all right and that sort of thing, I suppose?"

"They are nice people," I said emphatically. "He's a gentleman and they're devoted. He just looks like a big boy who's got into an awful mess and doesn't know how to get out. And she's backing him up. She's a dear."

"Humph!" said Mr. Patton. "Don't suppress any evidence because she's a dear and he's a handsome big boy!"

"I didn't say he was handsome," I snapped.

"Did you ever see a ghost or think you saw one?" he inquired suddenly.

"No, but one of my aunts has. Hers always carry their heads. She asked one a question once and the head nodded."

"Then you believe in things of that sort?"

"Not a particle—but I'm afraid of them."

He smiled, and shortly after that, I went back to the house. I think he was sorry about the ghost question, for he explained that he had been trying me out, and that I looked well in my cloak and bonnet.

"I'm afraid of your chin generally," he said; "but the white lawn ties have a softening effect. In view of the ties I have almost the courage—"

"Yes?"

"I think not, after all." he decided. "The chin is there, ties or no ties. Good night, and—for heaven's sake, don't run any unnecessary risks."

The change from his facetious tone to earnestness was so unexpected that I was still standing there on the pavement when he plunged into the darkness of the square and disappeared.

IV

At ten minutes after eight, I was back in the house. Mr. Reed admitted me, going through the tedious process of unlocking outer and inner vestibule doors and fastening them again behind me. He inquired politely if I had had a pleasant walk, and without waiting for my reply, fell to reading the evening paper. He seemed to have forgotten me absolutely. First, he scanned the headlines; then he turned feverishly to something farther on and ran his fingers down along a column. His lips were twitching, but evidently he did not find what he expected—or feared—for he threw the paper away and did not glance at it again. I watched him from the angle of the stairs.

Even for that short interval Mrs. Reed had taken his place at the children's door.

She wore a black dress, long-sleeved and high at the throat, instead of the silk negligee of the previous evening, and she held a book. But she was not reading. She smiled rather wistfully when she saw me.

"How fresh you always look!" she said. "And so self-reliant. I wish I had your courage."

"I am perfectly well. I dare say that explains a lot. Kiddies asleep?"

"Freddie isn't. He has been crying for Chang. I hate night, Miss Adams. I'm like Freddie. All my troubles come up about this time. I'm horribly depressed."

Her blue eyes filled with tears.

"I haven't been sleeping well," she confessed.

I should think not!

Without taking off my things I went down to Mr. Reed in the lower hall.

"I'm going to insist on something," I said. "Mrs. Reed is highly nervous. She says she has not been sleeping. I think if I give her an opiate, and she gets an entire night's sleep, it may save her a breakdown."

I looked straight in his eyes, and for once, he did evade me.

"I'm afraid I've been very selfish," he said. "Of course she must have sleep. I'll give you a powder, unless you have something you prefer to use."

I remembered then that he was a chemist, and said I would gladly use whatever he gave me.

"There is another thing I wanted to speak about, Mr. Reed," I said. "The children are mourning their dog. Don't you think he may have been accidentally shut up somewhere in the house in one of the upper floors?"

"Why do you say that?" he demanded sharply.

"They say they have heard him howling."

He hesitated for barely a moment. Then:

"Possibly," he said. "But they will not hear him again. The little chap has been sick, and he—died today. Of course the boys are not to know."

No one watched the staircase that night. I gave Mrs. Reed the opiate and saw her comfortably into bed. When I went back fifteen minutes later, she was resting, but not asleep. Opiates sometimes make people garrulous for a little while—sheer comfort, perhaps, and relaxed tension. I've had stockbrokers and bankers in the hospital give me tips, after a hypodermic of morphine, that would have made me

wealthy had I not been limited to my training allow-
ance of twelve dollars a month.

"I was just wondering," she said as I tucked her
up, "where a woman owes the most allegiance—to
her husband or to her children?"

"Why not split it up," I said cheerfully, "and try
doing what seems best for both?"

"But that's only a compromise!" she complained,
and was asleep almost immediately. I lowered the
light and closed the door, and shortly after I heard
Mr. Reed locking it from the outside.

With the bolt off my door and Mrs. Reed asleep,
my plan for the night was easily carried out. I went
to bed for a couple of hours and slept calmly. I
awakened once with the feeling that someone was
looking at me from the passage into the night nursery, but there was no one there. However, so strong
had been the feeling, that I got up and went into the
back room. The children were asleep, and all doors
opening into the hall were locked. But the window
on to the porte-cochère roof was open and the cur-
tain blowing. There was no one on the roof.

It was not twelve o'clock, and I still had an hour.
I went back to bed.

At one, I prepared to make a thorough search of
the house. Looking from one of my windows, I

thought I saw the shadowy figure of a man across the street, and I was comforted. Help was always close, I felt. And yet, as I stood inside my door in my rubber-soled shoes, with my ulster over my uniform and a revolver and my skeleton keys in my pockets, my heart was going very fast. The stupid story of the ghost came back and made me shudder, and the next instant, I was remembering Mrs. Reed the night before, staring down into the lower hall with fixed glassy eyes.

My plan was to begin at the top of the house and work down. The thing was the more hazardous, of course, because Mr. Reed was most certainly somewhere about. I had no excuse for being on the third floor. Down below I could say I wanted tea, or hot water—anything. But I did not expect to find Mr. Reed up above. The terror, whatever it was, seemed to lie below.

Access to the third floor was not easy. The main staircase did not go up. To get there I was obliged to unlock the door at the rear of the hall with my own keys. I was working in bright light, trying my keys one after another, and watching over my shoulder as I did so. When the door finally gave, it was a relief to slip into the darkness beyond, ghosts or no ghosts.

I am always a silent worker. Caution about closing doors and squeaking hinges is second nature to me. One learns to be cautious when one's only chance of sleep is not to rouse a peevish patient and have to give a body massage, as like as not, or listen to domestic troubles—"I said" and "he said"—until one is almost crazy.

So I made no noise. I closed the door behind me and stood blinking in the darkness. I listened. There was no sound above or below. Now houses at night have no terror for me. Every nurse is obliged to do more or less going about in the dark. But I was not easy. Suppose Mr. Reed should call me? True, I had locked my door and had the key in my pocket. But a dozen emergencies flew through my mind as I felt for the stair rail.

There was a curious odor through all the back staircase, a pungent, aromatic scent that, with all my familiarity with drugs, was strange to me. As I slowly climbed the stairs, it grew more powerful. The air was heavy with it, as though no windows had been opened in that part of the house. There was no door at the top of this staircase, as there was on the second floor. It opened into an upper hall, and across from the head of the stairs was a door leading into a room. This door was closed. On this staircase, as on all the others, the carpet had been newly lifted. My electric flash showed the white boards and painted borders, the carpet tacks, many of them still in place. One, lying loose, penetrated my rubber sole and went into my foot.

I sat down in the dark and took off the shoe. As I did so my flash, on the step beside me, rolled over and down with a crash. I caught it on the next step, but the noise had been like a pistol shot.

Almost immediately a voice spoke above me sharply. At first I thought it was out in the upper hall. Then I realized that the closed door was between it and me.

"Ees that you, Meester Reed?"

Mademoiselle!

"Meester Reed!" plaintively. "Eet comes up again, Meester Reed! I die! Tomorrow I die!"

She listened. On no reply coming she began to groan rhythmically, to a curious accompaniment of creaking. When I had gathered up my nerves again I realized that she must be sitting in a rocking chair. The groans were really little plaintive grunts.

By the time I had got my shoe on, she was up again, and I could hear her pacing the room, the heavy step of a woman well fleshed and not young. Now and then, she stopped inside the door and listened; once she shook the knob and mumbled querulously to herself.

I recovered the flash, and with infinite caution worked my way to the top of the stairs. Mademoiselle was locked in, doubly bolted in. Two strong bolts, above and below, supplemented the door lock.

Her ears must have been very quick, or else she felt my softly padding feet on the boards outside, for suddenly she flung herself against the door and begged for a priest, begged piteously, in jumbled French and English. She wanted food; she was dying of hunger. She wanted a priest.

And all the while I stood outside the door and wondered what I should do. Should I release the woman? Should I go down to the lower floor and get the detective across the street to come in and force the door? Was this the terror that held the house in thrall—this babbling old Frenchwoman calling for food and a priest in one breath?

Surely not. This was a part of the mystery, not all. The real terror lay below. It was not Mademoiselle, locked in her room on the upper floor, that the Reeds waited for at the top of the stairs. But why was Mademoiselle locked in her room? Why were the children locked in? What was this thing that had turned a home into a jail, a barracks, that had sent away the servants, imprisoned and probably killed the dog, sapped the joy of life from two young people? What was it that Mademoiselle cried "comes up again"?

I looked toward the staircase. Was it coming up the staircase?

I am not afraid of the thing I can see, but it seemed to me, all at once, that if anything was going to come up the staircase, I might as well get down first. A staircase is no place to meet anything, especially if one doesn't know what it is.

I listened again. Mademoiselle was quiet. I flashed my light down the narrow stairs. They were quite empty. I shut off the flash and went down. I tried to go slowly, to retreat with dignity, and by the time I had reached the landing below, I was heartily ashamed of myself. Was this shivering girl the young woman Mr. Patton called his right hand?

I dare say I should have stopped there, for that night at least. My nerves were frayed. But I forced myself on. The mystery lay below. Well, then, I was going down. It could not be so terrible. At least it was nothing supernatural. There must be a natural explanation. And then that silly story about the headless things must pop into my head and start me down trembling.

The lower rear staircase was black dark, like the upper, but just at the foot a light came in through a barred window. I could see it plainly and the shadows of the iron grating on the bare floor. I stood there listening. There was not a sound.

It was not easy to tell exactly what followed. I stood there with my hand on the rail. I'd been very silent; my rubber shoes attended to that. And one moment the staircase was clear, with a patch of light at the bottom. The next, something was there, half way down—a head, it seemed to be, with a pointed hood like a monk's cowl. There was no body. It seemed to lie at my feet. But it was living. It moved. I could tell the moment when the eyes lifted and saw my feet, the slow back-tilting of the head as they followed up my body. All the air was squeezed out of my lungs; a heavy hand seemed to press on my chest. I remember raising a shaking hand and flinging my flashlight at the head. The flash clattered on the stair tread harmless. Then the head was gone and something living slid over my foot.

I stumbled back to my room and locked the door. It was two hours before I had strength enough to get my aromatic ammonia bottle.

V

It seemed to me that I had hardly dropped asleep before the children were in the room, clamoring.

"The goldfish are dead!" Harry said, standing soberly by the bed. "They are all dead with their stummicks turned up."

I sat up. My head ached violently.

"They can't be dead, old chap." I was feeling about for my kimono, but I remembered that when I had found my way back to the nursery after my fright on the back stairs I had lain down in my uniform. I crawled out, hardly able to stand. "We gave them fresh water yesterday, and—"

I had got to the aquarium. Harry was right. The little darting flames of pink and gold were still. They floated about, rolling gently, as Freddie prodded them with a forefinger, dull-eyed, pale bellies up-turned. In his cage above, the little parrot watched out of a crooked eye.

I ran to the medicine closet in the bathroom. Freddie had a weakness for administering medicine. I had only just rescued the parrot from the result of his curiosity and a headache tablet the day before.

"What did you give them?" I demanded.

"Bread," said Freddie stoutly.

"Only bread?"

"Dirty bread," Harry put in. "I told him it was dirty."

"Where did you get it?"

"On the roof of the porte-cochère!"

Shade of Montessori! The rascals had been out on that sloping tin roof. It turned me rather sick to think of it.

Accused, they admitted it frankly.

"I unlocked the window," Harry said, "and Freddie got the bread. It was out in the gutter. He slipped once."

"Almost went over and made a squash on the pavement," added Freddie. "We gave the little fishes the bread for breakfast, and now they're gone to God."

The bread had contained poison, of course. Even the two little snails that crawled over the sand in the aquarium were motionless. I sniffed the water. It had a slightly foreign odor. I did not recognize it.

Panic seized me then. I wanted to get away and take the children with me. The situation was too hideous. But it was still early. I could only wait until the family roused. In the meantime, however, I made a nerve-racking excursion out on to the tin roof and down to the gutter. There was no more of the bread there. The porte-cochère was at the side of the house. As I stood balancing myself perilously on the edge, summoning my courage to climb back to the window above, I suddenly remembered the guard Mr. Patton had promised and glanced toward the square.

The guard was still there. More than that, he was running across the street toward me. It was Mr. Patton himself. He brought up between the two houses with absolute fury in his face.

"Go back!" he waved. "What are you doing out there anyhow? That roof's as slippery as the devil!"

I turned meekly and crawled back with as much dignity as I could. I did not say anything. There was nothing I could bawl from the roof. I could only close and lock the window and hope that the people in the next house still slept. Mr. Patton must have gone shortly after, for I did not see him again.

I wondered if he had relieved the night watch, or if he could possibly have been on guard himself all that chilly April night.

Mr. Reed did not breakfast with us. I made a point of being cheerful before the children, and their mother was rested and brighter than I had seen her. But more than once, I found her staring at me in a puzzled way. She asked me if I had slept.

"I wakened only once," she said. "I thought I heard a crash of some sort. Did you hear it?"

"What sort of a crash?" I evaded.

The children had forgotten the goldfish for a time. Now they remembered and clamored their news to her.

"Dead?" she said, and looked at me.

"Poisoned," I explained. "I shall nail the windows over the porte-cochère shut, Mrs. Reed. The boys got out there early this morning and picked up something—bread, I believe. They fed it to the fish and—they are dead."

All the light went out of her face. She looked tired and harassed as she got up.

"I wanted to nail the window," she said vaguely, "but Mr. Reed— Suppose they had eaten that bread, Miss Adams, instead of giving it to the fish!"

The same thought had chilled me with horror. We gazed at each other over the unconscious heads of the children, and my heart ached for her. I made a sudden resolution.

"When I first came," I said to her, "I told you I wanted to help. That's what I'm here for. But how am I to help either you or the children when I do not know what danger it is that threatens? It isn't fair to you, or to them, or even to me."

She was much shaken by the poison incident. I thought she wavered.

"Are you afraid the children will be stolen?"

"Oh, no."

"Or hurt in any way?" I was thinking of the bread on the roof.

"No."

"But you are afraid of something?"

Harry looked up suddenly.

"Mother's never afraid," he said stoutly.

I sent them both in to see if the fish were still dead.

"There is something in the house downstairs that you are afraid of?" I persisted.

She took a step forward and caught my arm.

"I had no idea it would be like this, Miss Adams. I'm dying of fear!"

I had a quick vision of the swathed head on the back staircase, and some of my night's terror came back to me. I believe we stared at each other with dilated pupils for a moment. Then I asked:

"Is it a real thing?—surely you can tell me this. Are you afraid of a reality, or—is it something supernatural?" I was ashamed of the question. It sounded so absurd in the broad light of that April morning.

"It is a real danger," she replied. Then I think she decided that she had gone as far as she dared, and I went through the ceremony of letting her out and of locking the door behind her.

The day was warm. I threw up some of the windows, and the boys and I played ball using a rolled handkerchief. My part, being to sit on the floor with a newspaper folded into a bat and to bang at the handkerchief as it flew past me, became automatic after a time.

As I look back, I see a pair of disordered young rascals in Russian blouses and bare round knees doing a great deal of yelling and some very crooked throwing; a nurse sitting tailor fashion on the floor, alternately ducking to save her cap and making vigorous but ineffectual passes at the ball with her newspaper bat. And I see sunshine in the room, and the dwarf parrot eating sugar out of his claw. And below, the fish in the aquarium floating belly-up with dull eyes.

Mr. Reed brought up our luncheon tray. He looked tired and depressed and avoided my eyes. I watched him while I spread the bread and butter for the children. He nailed shut the windows that opened on to the porte-cochère roof, and, when he thought I was not looking, he examined the registers in the wall to see if the gratings were closed. The boys put the dead fish in a box and made him promise a decent interment in the garden. They called on me for an epitaph, and I scrawled on top of the box:

> *These fish are dead*
> *Because a boy called Fred*
> *Went out on a porch roof when he should*
> *Have been in bed.*

I was much pleased with it. It seemed to me that an epitaph, which can do no good to the departed, should at least convey a moral. But to my horror Freddie broke into loud wails and would not be comforted.

It was three o'clock, therefore, before they were both settled for their afternoon naps, and I was free. I had determined to do one thing, and to do it in daylight—to examine the back staircase inch by inch. I knew I would be courting discovery, but the thing had to be done, and no power on earth would have made me essay such an investigation after dark.

It was all well enough for me to say to myself that there was a natural explanation; that this had been a human head, of a certainty; that something living and not spectral had slid over my foot in the darkness. I would not have gone back there again at night for youth, love, or money. But I did not investigate the staircase that day, after all.

I made a curious discovery after the boys had settled down in their small white beds. A venturesome fly had sailed in through an open window, and I was immediately in pursuit of him with my paper bat. Driven from the cornice to the chandelier, harried here, swatted there, finally he took refuge inside the furnace register.

Perhaps it is my training—I used to know how many million germs a fly packed about with it, and the generous benevolence with which it distributed them; I've forgotten—but the sight of a single fly maddens me. I said that to Mr. Patton once, and he

asked what the sight of a married one would do. So
I sat down by the register and waited. It was then
that I made the curious discovery that the furnace
downstairs was burning, and burning hard. A fierce
heat assailed me as I opened the grating. I drove the
fly out of cover, but I had no time for him. The
furnace going full on a warm spring day! It was
strange.

Perhaps I was stupid. Perhaps the whole thing
should have been clear to me. But it was not. I sat
there bewildered and tried to figure it out. I went
over it point by point:

The carpets up all over the house, lights going
full all night and doors locked.

The cot at the top of the stairs and Mrs. Reed
staring down.

The bolt outside my door to lock me in.

The death of Chang.

Mademoiselle locked in her room upstairs and
begging for a priest.

The poison on the porch roof.

The head without a body on the staircase and
the thing that slid over my foot.

The furnace going, and the thing I recognized as
I sat there beside the register—the unmistakable
odor of burning cloth.

Should I have known? I wonder. It looks so clear to me now.

I did not investigate the staircase, for the simple reason that my skeleton key, which unfastened the lock of the door at the rear of the second-floor hall, did not open the door. I did not understand at once and stood stupidly working with the lock. The door was bolted on the other side. I wandered as aimlessly as I could down the main staircase and tried the corresponding door on the lower floor. It, too, was locked. Here was an impasse for sure. As far as I could discover the only other entrance to the back staircase was through the window with the iron grating.

As I turned to go back, I saw my electric flash, badly broken, lying on a table in the hall. I did not claim it.

The lower floor seemed entirely deserted. The drawing room and library were in their usual disorder, undusted and bare of floor. The air everywhere was close and heavy; there was not a window open. I sauntered through the various rooms, picked up a book in the library as an excuse, and tried the door of the room behind. It was locked. I thought at first that something moved behind it, but if anything lived there, it did not stir again. And yet, I had a vivid impression that just on the other side of the door, ears as keen as mine were listening. It was broad day, but I backed away from the door and out into the wide hall. My nerves were still raw, no doubt, from the night before.

I was to meet Mr. Patton at half after seven that night, and when Mrs. Reed relieved me at seven, I had half an hour to myself. I spent it in Beauregard Gardens, with the dry fountain in the center. The place itself was charming, the trees still black but lightly fringed with new green, early spring flowers in the borders, neat paths and, bordering it all, the solid, dignified backs of the Beauregard houses. I sat down on the coping of the fountain and surveyed the Reed house. Those windows above were Mademoiselle's. The shades were drawn, but no light came through or round them. The prisoner—for prisoner she was by every rule of bolt and lock—must be sitting in the dark. Was she still begging for her priest? Had she had any food? Was she still listening inside her door for whatever it was that was coming up?

In all the other houses, windows were open; curtains waved gently in the spring air; the cheerful signs of the dinner hour were evident nearby—moving servants, a gleam of stately shirt bosom as a butler mixed a salad, a warm radiance of candlelight from dining room tables, and the reflected glow of flowers. Only the Reed house stood gloomy, unlighted, almost sinister.

Beauregard Place dined early. It was one of the traditions, I believe. It liked to get to the theater or the opera early, and it believed in allowing the servants a little time in the evenings. So, although it was only something after seven, the evening rite of the table crumbs began to be observed. Came a butler, bowed to me with a word of apology, and dumped the contents of a silver tray into the basin; came a pretty girl, flung her crumbs gracefully and smiled with a flash of teeth at the butler.

Then for five minutes I was alone.

It was Nora, the girl we had met on the street, who came next. She saw me and came round to me with a little air of triumph.

"Well, I'm back in the square again, after all, miss," she said. "And a better place than the Reeds. I don't have the doilies to do."

"I'm very glad you are settled again, Nora."

She lowered her voice.

"I'm just trying it out," she observed. "The girl that left said I wouldn't stay. She was scared off. There have been some queer doings—not that I believe in ghosts or anything like that. But my mother in the old country had the second-sight, and if there's anything going on I'll be right sure to see it."

It took encouragement to get her story, and it was secondhand at that, of course. But it appeared that a state of panic had seized the Beauregard servants. The alarm was all downstairs and had been started by a cook who, coming in late and going to the basement to prepare herself a cup of tea, had found her kitchen door locked and a light going beyond. Suspecting another maid of violating the tea canister she had gone soft-footed to the outside of the house and had distinctly seen a gray figure crouching in a corner of the room. She had called the butler, and they had made an examination of the entire basement without result. Nothing was missing from the house.

"And that figure has been seen again and again, miss," Nora finished. "McKenna's butler, Joseph, saw it in this very spot, walking without a sound and the street light beyond there shining straight through it. Over in the Smythe house, the laundress, coming in late and going down to the basement to soak her clothes for the morning, met the thing on the basement staircase and fainted dead away."

I had listened intently.

"What do they think it is?" I asked.

She shrugged her shoulders and picked up her tray.

"I'm not trying to say, and I guess nobody is. But if there's been a murder, it's pretty well known that the ghost walks about until the burial service is read and it's properly buried."

She glanced at the Reed house.

"For instance," she demanded, "where is Mademoiselle?"

"She is alive," I said rather sharply. "And even if what you say were true, what in the world would make her wander about the basements? It seems so silly, Nora, a ghost haunting damp cellars and laundries with stationary tubs and all that."

"Well," she contended, "it seems silly for them to sit on cold tombstones—and yet that's where they generally sit, isn't it?"

Mr. Patton listened gravely to my story that night.

"I don't like it," he said when I had finished. "Of course, the head on the staircase is nonsense. Your nerves were ragged, and our eyes play tricks on all of us. But as for the Frenchwoman—"

"If you accept her, you must accept the head," I snapped. "It was there—it was a head without a body—and it looked up at me."

We were walking through a quiet street, and he bent over and caught my wrist.

"Pulse racing," he commented. "I'm going to take you away, that's certain. I can't afford to lose my best assistant. You're too close, Miss Adams; you've lost your perspective."

"I've lost my temper!" I retorted. "I shall not leave until I know what this thing is, unless you choose to ring the doorbell and tell them I'm a spy."

He gave in when he saw that I was firm, but not without a final protest.

"I'm directly responsible for you to your friends," he said. "There's probably a young man somewhere who will come gunning for me if anything happens to you. And I don't care to be gunned for. I get enough of that in my regular line."

"There is no young man," I said shortly.

"Have you been able to see the cellars?"

"No, everything is locked off."

"Do you think the rear staircase goes all the way down?"

"I haven't the slightest idea."

"You are in the house. Have you any suggestions as to the best method of getting into the house? Is Reed on guard all night?"

"I think he is."

"It may interest you to know," he said finally, "that I sent a reliable man to break in there last night quietly, and that he—couldn't do it. He got a leg through a cellar window, and came near not getting it out again. Reed was just inside in the dark." He laughed a little, but I guessed that the thing galled him.

"I do not believe that he would have found anything if he had succeeded in getting in. There has been no crime, Mr. Patton, I am sure of that. But there is a menace of some sort in the house."

"Then why does Mrs. Reed stay and keep the children if there is danger?"

"I believe she is afraid to leave him. There are times when I think that he is desperate."

"Does he ever leave the house?"

"I think not, unless—"

"Yes?"

"Unless he is the basement ghost of the other houses."

He stopped in his slow walk and considered it.

"It's possible. In that case, I could have him waylaid tonight in the gardens and left there, tied. It would be a hold-up, you understand. The police have no excuse for coming in yet. Or, if we found him breaking into one of the other houses, we could get him there. He'd be released, of course, but it would give us time. I want to clean the thing up. I'm not easy while you are in that house."

We agreed that I was to wait inside one of my windows that night, and that on a given signal, I should go down and open the front door. The whole thing, of course, was contingent on Mr. Reed leaving the house sometime that night. It was only a chance.

"The house is barred like a fortress," Mr. Patton said as he left me. "The window with the grating is hopeless. We tried it last night."

VI

I find that my notes of that last night in the house on Beauregard Square are rather confused, some written at the time, some just before. For instance, on the edge of a newspaper clipping I find this:

"Evidently, this is the item. R— went pale on reading it. Did not allow wife to see paper."

The clipping is an account of the sudden death of an elderly gentleman named Smythe, one of the Beauregard families.

The next clipping is less hasty and is on a yellow symptom record. It has been much folded—I believe I tucked it in my apron belt:

"If the rear staircase is bolted everywhere from the inside, how did the person who locked it, either Mr. or Mrs. Reed, get back into the body of the house again? Or did Mademoiselle do it? In that case, she is no longer a prisoner, and the bolts outside her room are not fastened.

"At eleven o'clock tonight, Harry wakened with earache. I went to the kitchen to heat some mullein oil and laudanum. Mrs. Reed was with the boy, and Mr. Reed was not in sight. I slipped into the library and used my skeleton keys on the locked door to the rear room. It was empty even of furniture, but there is a huge box there, with a lid that fastens down with steel hooks. The lid is full of small air holes. I had no time to examine further.

"It is one o'clock. Harry is asleep and his mother is dozing across the foot of his bed. I have found the way to get to the rear staircase. There are outside steps from the basement to the garden. The staircase goes down all the way to the cellar evidently. Then the lower door in the cellar must be only locked, not bolted from the inside. I shall try to get to the cellar."

The next is a scrawl:

"Cannot get to the outside basement steps. Mr. Reed is wandering round lower floor. I reported

Harry's condition and came up again. I must get to the back staircase."

I wonder if I have been able to convey, even faintly, the situation in that highly respectable old house that night: The fear that hung over it, a fear so great that even I, an outsider and stout of nerve, felt it and grew cold; the unnatural brilliancy of light that bespoke dread of the dark; the hushed voices, the locked doors and staring, peering eyes; the babbling Frenchwoman on an upper floor, the dead fish, the dead dog. And, always in my mind, that vision of dread on the back staircase and the thing that slid over my foot.

At two o'clock, I saw Mr. Patton, or whoever was on guard in the park across the street, walk quickly toward the house and disappear round the corner toward the gardens in the rear. There had been no signal, but I felt sure that Mr. Reed had left the house. His wife was still asleep across Harry's bed. As I went out, I locked the door behind me, and I took also the key to the night nursery. I thought that something disagreeable, to say the least, was inevitable, and why let her in for it?

The lower hall was lighted as usual and empty. I listened, but there were no restless footsteps. I did not like the lower hall. Only a thin wooden door stood between me and the rear staircase, and anyone who thinks about the matter will realize that a door is no barrier to a head that can move about without a body. I am afraid I looked over my shoulder while I unlocked the front door, and I know I breathed better when I was out in the air.

I wore my dark ulster over my uniform, and I had my revolver and keys. My flash, of course, was useless. I missed it horribly. But to get to the staircase was an obsession by that time, in spite of my fear of it, to find what it guarded, to solve its mystery. I worked round the house, keeping close to the wall, until I reached the garden. The night was the city night, never absolutely dark. As I hesitated at the top of the basement steps, it seemed to me that figures were moving about among the trees.

The basement door was unlocked and open. I was not prepared for that, and it made me, if anything, more uneasy. I had a box of matches with me, and I wanted light as a starving man wants food. But I dared not light them. I could only keep a tight grip on my courage and go on. A small passage first, with whitewashed stone walls, cold and scaly under my hand; then a large room, and still darkness. Worse than darkness, something crawling and scratching round the floor.

I struck my match, then, and it seemed to me that something white flashed into a corner and disappeared. My hands were shaking, but I managed to light a gas jet and to see that I was in the laundry. The staircase came down here, narrower than above, and closed off with a door.

The door was closed and there was a heavy bolt on it but no lock.

And now, with the staircase accessible and a gaslight to keep up my courage, I grew brave, almost reckless. I would tell Mr. Patton all about this cellar, which his best men had not been able to enter. I would make a sketch for him—coal-bins, laundry tubs, everything. Foolish, of course, but hold the gas jet responsible—the reckless bravery of light after hideous darkness.

So I went on, forward. The glow from the laundry followed me. I struck matches, found potatoes and cases of mineral water, bruised my knees on a discarded bicycle, stumbled over a box of soap. Twice out of the corner of my eye and never there when I looked, I caught the white flash that had frightened me before. Then, at last, I brought up before a door and stopped. It was a curiously barricaded door, nailed against disturbance by a plank fastened across, and, as if to make intrusion without discovery impossible, pasted round every crack and over the keyhole with strips of strong yellow paper. It was an ominous door. I wanted to run away from it, and I wanted also desperately to stand and look at it and imagine what might lie beyond. Here, again, was the strange, spicy odor that I had noticed in the back staircase.

I think it is indicative of my state of mind that I backed away from the door. I did not turn and run. Nothing in the world would have made me turn my back to it.

Somehow or other, I got back into the laundry and jerked myself together.

It was ten minutes after two. I had been just ten minutes in the basement!

The staircase daunted me in my shaken condition. I made excuses for delaying my venture, looked for another box of matches, listened at the end of the passage, finally slid the bolts and opened the door. The silence was impressive. In the laundry, there were small, familiar sounds—the dripping of water from a faucet, the muffled measure of a gas meter, the ticking of a clock on the shelf. To leave it all, to climb into that silence—

Lying on the lower step was a curious instrument. It was a sort of tongs made of steel, about

two feet long, and fastened together like a pair of
scissors, the joint about five inches from the flat-
tened ends. I carried it to the light and examined it.
One end was smeared with blood and short,
brownish hairs. It made me shudder, but—from that
time on, I think I knew. Not the whole story, of
course, but somewhere in the back of my head, as I
climbed in that hideous quiet, the explanation was
developing itself. I did not think it out. It worked
itself out as, step after step, match after match, I
climbed the staircase.

Up to the first floor there was nothing. The landing was bare of carpet. I was on the first floor now.
On each side, doors, carefully bolted, led into the
house. I opened the one into the hall and listened. I
had been gone from the children fifteen minutes and
they were on my mind. But everything was quiet.

The sight of the lights and the familiar hall gave
me courage. After all, if I was right, what could the
head on the staircase have been but an optical delusion? And I was right. The evidence—the tongs—
was in my hand. I closed and bolted the door and
felt my way back to the stairs. I lighted no matches
this time. I had only a few, and on this landing there
was a little light from the grated window, although
the staircase above was in black shadow.

I had one foot on the lowest stair, when suddenly overhead came the thudding of hands on a
closed door. It broke the silence like an explosion. It
sent chills up and down my spine. I could not move
for a moment. It was the Frenchwoman!

I believe I thought of fire. The idea had obsessed
me in that house of locked doors. I remember a
strangling weight of fright on my chest and of trying
to breathe. Then I started up the staircase, running as
fast as I could lift my weighted feet, I remember that,
and getting up perhaps a third of the way. Then there
came a plunging forward into space, my hands out, a
shriek frozen on my lips, and—quiet.

I do not think I fainted. I know I was always
conscious of my arm doubled under me, a pain,
and darkness. I could hear myself moaning, but
almost as if it were someone else. There were other
sounds, but they did not concern me much. I was
not even curious about my location. I seemed to be
a very small consciousness surrounded by a great
deal of pain.

Several centuries later, a light came and leaned
over me from somewhere above. Then the light said:

"Here she is!"

"Alive?" I knew that voice, but I could not think
whose it was.

"I'm not— Yes, she's moaning."

They got me out somewhere, and I believe I still clung to the tongs. I had fallen on them and had a cut on my chin. I could stand, I found, although I swayed. There was plenty of light now in the back hallway, and a man I had never seen was investigating the staircase.

"Four steps off," he said. "Risers and treads gone and the supports sawed away. It's a trap of some sort."

Mr. Patton was examining my broken arm and paid no attention. The man let himself down into the pit under the staircase. When he straightened, only his head rose above the steps. Although I was white with pain to the very lips, I laughed hysterically.

"The head!" I cried. Mr. Patton swore under his breath.

They half led, half carried me into the library. Mr. Reed was there, with a detective on guard over him. He was sitting in his old position, bent forward, chin in palms. In the blaze of light, he was a pitiable figure, smeared with dust, disheveled from what had evidently been a struggle. Mr. Patton put me in a chair and dispatched one of the two men for the nearest doctor.

"This young lady," he said curtly to Mr. Reed, "fell into that damnable trap you made in the rear staircase."

"I locked off the staircase—but I am sorry she is hurt. My—my wife will be shocked. Only I wish you'd tell me what all this is about. You can't arrest me for going into a friend's house."

"If I send for some member of the Smythe family, will they acquit you?"

"Certainly they will," he said. "I—I've been raised with the Smythes. You can send for anyone you like." But his tone lacked conviction.

Mr. Patton made me as comfortable as possible, and then, sending the remaining detective out into the hall, he turned to his prisoner.

"Now, Mr. Reed," he said. "I want you to be sensible. For some days, a figure has been seen in the basements of the various Beauregard houses. Your friends, the Smythes, reported it. Tonight we are on watch, and we see you breaking into the basement of the Smythe house. We already know some curious things about you, such as dismissing all the servants on half an hour's notice and the disappearance of the French governess."

"Mademoiselle! Why, she—" He checked himself.

"When we bring you here tonight, and you ask to be allowed to go upstairs and prepare your wife, she is locked in. The nurse is missing. We find her at last, also locked away and badly hurt, lying in a staircase trap, where someone, probably yourself, has removed the steps. I do not want to arrest you, but, now I've started, I'm going to get to the bottom of all this."

Mr. Reed was ghastly, but he straightened in his chair.

"The Smythes reported this thing, did they?" he asked. "Well, tell me one thing. What killed the old gentleman—old Smythe?"

"I don't know."

"Well, go a little further." His cunning was boyish, pitiful. "How did he die? Or don't you know that either?"

Up to this point I had been rather a detached part of the scene, but now my eyes fell on the tongs beside me.

"Mr. Reed," I said, "isn't this thing too big for you to handle by yourself?"

"What thing?"

"You know what I mean. You've protected yourself well enough, but even if the—the thing you know of did not kill old Mr. Smythe, you cannot tell what will happen next."

"I've got almost all of them," he muttered sullenly. "Another night or two and I'd have had the lot."

"But even then the mischief may go on. It means a crusade; it means rousing the city. Isn't it the square thing now to spread the alarm?"

Mr. Patton could stand the suspense no longer.

"Perhaps, Miss Adams," he said, "you will be good enough to let me know what you are talking about."

Mr. Reed looked up at him with heavy eyes.

"Rats," he said. "They got away, twenty of them, loaded with bubonic plague."

I went to the hospital the next morning. Mr. Patton thought it best. There was no one in my little flat to look after me, and although the pain in my arm subsided after the fracture was set, I was still shaken.

He came the next afternoon to see me. I was propped up in bed, with my hair braided down in two pigtails and great hollows under my eyes.

"I'm comfortable enough," I said, in response to his inquiry; "but I'm feeling all of my years. This is my birthday. I am thirty today."

"I wonder," he said reflectively, "if I ever reach the mature age of one hundred, if I will carry in my head as many odds and ends of information as you have at thirty!"

"I?"

"You. How in the world did you know, for instance, about those tongs?"

"It was quite simple. I'd seen something like them in the laboratory here. Of course, I didn't know what animals he'd used, but the grayish brown hair looked like rats. The laboratory must be the cellar room. I knew it had been fumigated—it was sealed with paper, even over the keyhole."

So, sitting there beside me, Mr. Patton told me the story as he had got it from Mr. Reed—a tale of the offer in an English scientific journal of a large reward from some plague-ridden country of the East for an anti-plague serum. Mr. Reed had been working along bacteriological lines in his basement laboratory, mostly with guinea pigs and tuberculosis. He was in debt; the offer loomed large.

"He seems to think he was on the right track," Mr. Patton said. "He had twenty of the creatures in deep zinc cans with perforated lids. He says the disease is spread by fleas that infest the rats. So he had muslin as well over the lids. One can had infected rats, six of them. Then one day the Frenchwoman tried to give the dog a bath in a laundry tub and the dog bolted. The laboratory door was open in some way and he ran between the cans, upsetting them. Every rat was out in an instant. The Frenchwoman was frantic. She shut the door and tried to drive the things back. One bit her on the foot. The dog was not bitten, but there was the question of fleas.

"Well, the rats got away, and Mademoiselle retired to her room to die of plague. She was a loyal old soul; she wouldn't let them call a doctor. It would mean exposure, and after all, what could the doctors do? Reed used his serum and she's alive.

"Reed was frantic. His wife would not leave. There was the Frenchwoman to look after, and I think she was afraid he would do something desperate. They did the best they could, under the circumstances, for the children. They burned most of the carpets for fear of fleas, and put poison everywhere. Of course he had traps too.

"He had brass tags on the necks of the rats, and he got back a few—the uninfected ones. The other ones were probably dead. But he couldn't stop at that. He had to be sure that the trouble had not spread. And to add to their horror, the sewer along the street was being re-laid, and they had an influx of rats into the house. They found them everywhere in the lower floor. They even climbed the stairs. He says that the night you came, he caught a big fellow on the front staircase. There was always the danger that the fleas that carry the trouble had deserted the dead creatures for new fields. They took up all the rest of the carpets and burned them. To add to the general misery, the dog Chang developed unmistakable symptoms and had to be killed."

"But the broken staircase?" I asked. "And what was it that Mademoiselle said was coming up?"

"The steps were up for two reasons: The rats could not climb up, and beneath the steps, Reed says he caught in a trap two of the tagged ones. As for Mademoiselle, the thing that was coming up was her temperature—pure fright. The head you saw was poor Reed himself, wrapped in gauze against trouble and baiting his traps. He caught a lot in the neighbors' cellars and some in the garden."

"But why," I demanded, "why didn't he make it all known?"

Mr. Patton laughed while he shrugged his shoulders.

"A man hardly cares to announce that he has menaced the health of a city."

"But that night when I fell—was it only last night?—someone was pounding above. I thought there was a fire."

"The Frenchwoman had seen us waylay Reed from her window. She was crazy."

"And the trouble is over now?"

"Not at all," he replied cheerfully. "The trouble may be only beginning. We're keeping Reed's name out, but the Board of Health has issued a general warning. Personally I think his six pets died without passing anything along."

"But there was a big box with a lid—"

"Ferrets," he assured me. "Nice white ferrets with pink eyes and a taste for rats." He held out a thumb, carefully bandaged. "Reed had a couple under his coat when we took him in the garden. Probably one ran over your foot that night when you surprised him on the back staircase."

I went pale. "But if they are infected!" I cried; "and you are bitten—"

"The first thing a nurse should learn," he bent forward smiling, "is not to alarm her patient."

"But you don't understand the danger," I said despairingly. "Oh, if only men had a little bit of sense!"

"I must do something desperate then? Have the thumb cut off, perhaps?"

I did not answer. I lay back on my pillows with my eyes shut. I had given him the plague, had seen him die and be buried, before he spoke again.

"The chin," he said, "is not so firm as I had thought. The outlines are savage, but the dimple— You poor little thing; are you really frightened?"

"I don't like you," I said furiously. "But I'd hate to see anyone with—with that trouble."

"Then I'll confess. I was trying to take your mind off your troubles. The bite is there, but harmless. Those were new ferrets; had never been out."

I did not speak to him again. I was seething with indignation. He stood for a time looking down at me; then, unexpectedly, he bent over and touched his lips to my bandaged arm.

"Poor arm!" he said. "Poor, brave little arm!" Then he tiptoed out of the room. His very back was sheepish.

About the Author

Dubbed the American Agatha Christie, Mary Roberts Rinehart was born in Pittsburgh in 1876. The author of more than three dozen novels, many of them best-sellers, she was also a prolific writer of plays and short stories, and several of her works were adapted for film and television. She died in New York in 1958.

To see our other great titles,
visit us at:

Milton Keynes UK
Ingram Content Group UK Ltd.
UKHW012148090624
443713UK00001B/3

9 781610 530453